Candiss Diamondis

DIBU

Candiss Diamondis

Dibu the dung beetle was hunting for dung
for his family to feast on, and a nest for his young.
He ambled along then jumped up with glee,
screeching with excitement, "What's this I see?!"

Just up ahead on the dusty dirt road
lay the hugest brown poo, a fresh, smelly load.
He quickened his pace to get to his prize
before those bothersome blue-bottomed flies.

He gave some a sniff..

..and a lick just to taste..

..and the yumminess ZINGED

from his tongue to his waist.

Rolling some up in the roundest of balls,
    he set off home through Victoria Falls.

Now dung beetles have the most interesting way
of moving the dung to their homes far away.
The sun, wind and stars guide them along,
showing them 'This way!', and 'That way is wrong!'.

HOME

He lined himself up on the path up ahead,
then turned himself over...
"Let's go!" Dibu said.

He hummed as he rolled, and he rolled, and he rolled
as his sensational day began to unfold.

He hadn't gone far when he heard a strange sound,
so he stopped in his tracks and turned right around.

hmmmm hmmmm hmmmm

kreeee!
kreeee!
kreeee!

It was a shrilling, shrieking, chattering screecher...

Look at her here, this magnificent creature!

Feathered and plump, not a stork or an owl,
but a spotty and dotty grey guinea fowl.

The guinea hen scuttled around for some food,
then startled by Dibu, ran off with her brood.

They dashed off with speed through the bushes together.
Oh! What's this they left?

The most beautiful feather!

Dibu was thrilled; his wife would just love it,
so into the dung he proceeded to shove it.

He set off again with his ball and his feather,
straining a bit in the hot midday weather.

phoo, phoo, phoo

Through the still of the air came a soft, cooling breeze
and the heat on his back started to ease.
The wind came in gusts, so he looked up, quite curious...

Look at this here, this winged thing so glorious!

A dazzling butterfly fluttered just there,
then slowly she landed, gently, with care.

Her wings gave a beat and she left him in awe
as she danced a few steps on top of his ball.

She took off again with a quick gust of air,
and he noticed she'd left some footprints up there.
On closer inspection, he saw it was pollen –
a glistening gold she had coloured his dung in.
Dibu gasped in delight and clambered back down.
His dung was becoming the fanciest in town.

Onwards he went with his funky new ball,
whistling along to the fish eagles call.

WhewOO OOO

ooo ooo

He picked up some speed, rolling and rolling,
    when a smell drifted by. It was quite overwhelming!

A scent so intriguing, what could it be?

Look at this here,
		this spectacular tree!

A baobab stood there, in all of her glory.
Gnarly and twisted, a great double storey.
Covered in leaves, and dotted with flowers;
blossoms so splendid, but EW!
		their smell overpowers.

One fluttered down
and landed just
there,
so Dibu dashed over
and held it with care.
Velvety soft, airy
and free,
the most perfect of
gifts from the
baobab tree.

Dibu set off again, pleased with his flower,
up a wee hill he pushed with more power.

oomph, oomph, oomph.

At the top of the hill, he paused with his prize,
as something quite sparkly shone in his eyes.

Too glittery and glam for bark or a bone...

Look at this here, this shiny black stone!

The afternoon sun hit it just right,
to make it sparkle with luminous light.

Over he wandered and grabbed it with glee.
Dibu exclaimed, "You're coming with me!"
Carrying the jewel not all that small,
he planted it right on top of his ball.

On the final stretch home with his glamorous poo,
there was just one thing he still had to do...

Dibu climbed up a rock to take in the sight
of Victoria Falls – a sensory delight!

He lifted his head to admire this wonder –
the rushing of water that rumbled like thunder,
and felt the soft cool of the fine, misty spray,
as he breathed in the smell of fresh summer rain.

As evening set in, he continued on home.
The sun was now setting, the sky a pink chrome.
He steadily rolled, back to his wife,
pushing his prize, the best of their life.

His wife had been digging a hole in the ground
and looked up to see all the things he had found.

He told her his tales as they buried the treasure
then laid out the flower, the stone and the feather.
They sat down together beneath the full moon,
and Dibu, contented, began humming his tune.

There are lots of little creatures in this book!

Can you find the Little Five?

These are the fascinating little critters that share part of their name with the Big Five.

 Rhino beetle

 Elephant shrew

 Adult (looks a bit like a dragonfly!)

Ant lion

 Larva (eat LOTS of ants!)

 Leopard tortoise

 Buffalo weaver

And my Ubiquitous Five?

Big word! 'yoo-bik-wa-tis', meaning that they seem to be everywhere. You'll commonly find these creatures in the African bush.

 Hornbill

 Guinea fowl

 Dung beetle

 Impala

 Fish eagle

Dung beetles are truly remarkable creatures. Here are a few facts about them, that you may find quite interesting!

- There are over 7000 different species of dung beetles, and they are found on all continents except Antarctica.

- Dung beetles are grouped into rollers, tunnellers, dwellers and stealers. Dibu is a roller – they roll the dung into a ball, then move it away before burying it.

- They have SUPER strength! They can push a ball of dung 50 times their own weight.

- They also have a super sensitive sense of smell and can find a fresh ball of dung within minutes of it being dropped.

- Once they have rolled up a ball of dung, dung beetles move in straight lines away from the pile as quickly as possible before a 'stealer' grabs their ball! They do this by detecting straight lines of light from around the sun, moon and stars.

- Dung beetles eat the dung, and females bury their eggs in it so there is a delicious meal waiting when the eggs hatch.

- Dung beetles are the clean-up crew of the bush. By breaking up, moving and burying the dung, they prevent build-up of dung and flies, and they move nutrients through the ecosystem – it's a great fertilizer!